OUT in GAS

VICKI C. HAYES

SADDLEBACK
EDUCATIONAL PUBLISHING

red rhino
b⚭k s™

Body Switch	The Hero of	Sky Watchers
Clan Castles	Crow's Crossing	Standing by Emma
The Code	I Am Underdog	Starstruck
Fish Boy	Killer Flood	Stolen Treasure
Flyer	Little Miss Miss	The Soldier
Fight School	The Lost House	Too Many Dogs
The Garden Troll	The Love Mints	Zombies!
Ghost Mountain	**Out of Gas**	Zuze and the Star
The Gift	Racer	

With more titles on the way …

SADDLEBACK
EDUCATIONAL PUBLISHING
www.sdlback.com

ISBN-13: 978-1-62250-917-1
ISBN-10: 1-62250-917-X
eBook: 978-1-63078-169-9

Printed in Guangzhou, China
NOR/0215/CA21500098

19 18 17 16 15   1 2 3 4 5

TREY

Age: 11

Personality: friendly, happy, and a little shy

Future Goal: to be a professional soccer player in Europe

Favorite Food: raspberry jelly doughnuts

Best Quality: motivated to help others

THE TOOZERS

Age: 8 (in Earth years)

Secret Wish: to visit Twinsburg, Ohio, during their time on Earth

Favorite Activity: chasing comets

Upcoming Event: Poz has to get glasses

Best Quality: versatility

1
NO IDEA

"I hate school!" said Trey. "I want to play soccer. But Mister Dean says no. He wants me off the team."

"Why?" asked Dad.

Trey grabbed a warm loaf of bread. He stuffed it in a bag. He plopped the bag on a shelf.

GLUTEN FREE

"He wants my idea," said Trey. "For the sixth grade science fair. I need an idea by

Monday. Or I'm off the team." Trey dusted flour off his hands. He was helping his parents. They owned a bake shop.

"Easy," said Mom. "You like science." She took more bread out of the oven.

"That's right," said Dad. "You like space. How about looking at a new planet?" Dad was mixing dough.

"Or spaceships?" said Mom. "Or aliens?"

Trey grabbed another loaf of fresh bread.

"Those are no good," he said. "I have to test something. Or show how something works." He shoved the bread into a bag. He was mad. Mom looked at the squashed bread.

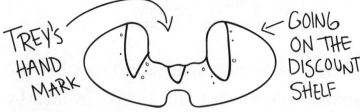

TREY'S HAND MARK

← GOING ON THE DISCOUNT SHELF

"Take a break," she said. "Take Max for a walk. Maybe you'll think of an idea."

Trey nodded. He dropped the bread on the table. He walked through the shop's back door. He walked into the house kitchen. The shop and the house were connected.

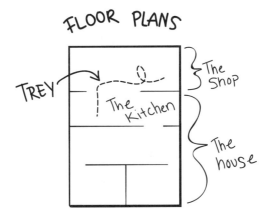

FLOOR PLANS

TREY

The Kitchen

The Shop

The house

"Let's go, Max," he called. The big dog ran up. "Let's go for a walk."

Trey liked walking with Max. He could tell his worries to Max. Trey and Max left the house. They headed into the woods.

"What will I do?" Trey asked Max. "I need an idea. I really want to play soccer. The science fair is stupid."

Max stuck his nose into some dead leaves. Then Max looked up. He pricked up his ears. Trey looked up. He saw a bright streak of light. It flashed across the sky. Then there was a loud crash. It came from up ahead.

Trey felt a wave of heat. Something had just happened.

"What was that?" asked Trey.

"Woof! Woof!" Max barked.

"I don't know either," said Trey. "Let's go see."

Trey ran through the woods. Max ran with him. Then they stopped. The woods looked odd.

"What is this?" asked Trey. He looked around. Many trees were gone. Some were broken. Some were smoking. Branches were on the ground. Leaves were in the air. The ground was smoking.

Then Trey saw a new thing. It didn't belong in the woods. It was a large box. It was silver. It looked like a big oven. Like the oven in the bake shop. It was stuck in the ground.

"I think it crashed," said Trey. "It crashed hard."

Max whined. He sniffed the air. He wanted to sniff the box. Trey grabbed Max.

"Don't go too close," said Trey. "It doesn't look safe. It might be hot. It might even blow up!"

2

THE CRASH

Trey stood under the trees. He kept Max close. He talked softly to Max.

"What is this box?" asked Trey. "Is it a spy plane?"

Max sniffed the air. Trey held him close.

"Is it from NASA?" asked Trey. "Is it a spaceship? Maybe it was going to the space station. And then it crashed. Maybe not. It's so small. Spaceships are bigger."

NORMAL-SIZED SPACESHIP

THE BOX

7

Trey stopped talking. He saw something new. The box had a door. The door was opening. Something came out. Two things. They oozed out. They looked like blobs.

"I was right," said Trey softly. "It is a spaceship. But it's not from Earth!"

Trey looked at the blobs. He thought of an old game. It was a video game. The game had ghosts in it. These blobs looked like those ghosts.

Then Max barked. He pulled away from Trey. He ran to the ship. He barked at the blobs. The blobs looked at Max. They shimmered. They stretched. They changed. The blobs changed into copies of Max!

Trey stared. He was so surprised. Now there were three dogs. They all looked like Max! How did the blobs do that?

The dogs met. They sniffed each other. Trey got mad. No one was going to hurt Max. Trey ran out of the trees.

"Stop!" he yelled. "Don't touch my dog!"

But which dog was Max? Trey wasn't sure. He called Max. All the dogs looked at Trey. Then one dog wagged its tail. That dog came to Trey. It was Max.

The other two dogs shimmered. They stretched. They changed. The dogs changed into … Trey! Trey was looking at two more Treys!

"Oh my gosh!" he said.

"Oh my gosh!" said the other two Treys.

3
TOOZERS

Max looked at the two new boys. He wagged his tail. But Trey was not happy. He grabbed Max. He frowned at the boys.

FUN DOG FACT:

- TAIL WAGGING TO THE **RIGHT** INDICATES -POSITIVE- EMOTIONS

- TAIL WAGGING TO THE **LEFT** INDICATES NEGATIVE EMOTIONS

"Who are you?" asked Trey. "Where are you from?"

"I am Neg," said one boy.

"I am Poz," said the other boy. "We are from Tooze."

"What is Tooze?" asked Trey. He kept Max close. He was not sure about the boys.

"Tooze is our home," said Poz. "We live there."

FROM A GALAXY THAT LOOKS LIKE A LARGE PIZZA

"It is a small planet," said Neg. "It is far away from here." Neg moved close to Poz. He looked at Trey's dog. "Is that your twin?" he asked Trey.

Trey looked at Max. He looked at the twin boys.

"I don't have a twin," said Trey.

"Everyone on Tooze has a twin," said Poz.

"Earth is not the same as Tooze," said

Trey. He looked at the boys. "Why are you here?" he asked.

"Our ship stopped," said Poz. "We don't know why."

"It broke," said Neg. "We had to land. We did not want to. We do not want to be on Earth."

THEY MISS THEIR GIRLFRIENDS

"Can you fix your ship?" asked Trey. "Do you need help?"

"No," said Neg. "We don't need help."

"Maybe," said Poz. "Maybe we need help."

"Tell me what happened," Trey said.

Poz looked at Neg. Neg nodded.

"Our ship runs on gas," said Poz. "The gas is made by yeets. But the yeets stopped. They stopped making gas."

"What are yeets?" asked Trey.

Poz went in the ship. He came out. He had a bin.

"These are yeets," he said. Poz gave the bin to Trey. Trey looked inside. The yeets were in a pile. They looked like white sand. But they were moving.

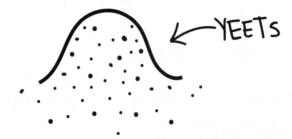

Max sniffed the yeets. Max sneezed. Trey watched the yeets blow around. Then they moved back into a pile.

"Are they okay?" asked Trey.

"They are fine," said Poz.

"But something is wrong," said Neg. "We had to land on Earth. We are stuck here."

Poz took the yeets. He went back in the ship. He came out. He looked sad.

"I know what's wrong," said Poz. "The mish is gone."

"Mish?" said Trey. "What's mish?"

"Mish is food," said Poz. "The yeets eat mish."

"Why is it gone?" asked Trey.

"The tank has a hole," said Poz. "Now the mish is gone. It is in space."

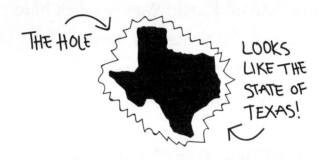

THE HOLE

LOOKS LIKE THE STATE OF TEXAS!

"I told you," said Neg. "We are stuck on Earth."

"No," said Poz. "We just have to find more mish."

"Earth has no mish," said Neg.

"Maybe it does," said Poz. "We will look."

"I can help," said Trey. "But tell me. What is mish?"

"Mish is food," said Poz. Trey put his hands on his hips.

"Yes," said Trey. "But what is it called on Earth?"

"We don't know," said Poz.

"What does it look like?" asked Trey.

"It looks like mish," said Neg.

Trey was fed up. He wanted to help the Toozers. But he didn't know how.

"We will look for mish now," said Poz.

The Toozers looked at the ground. They looked up at the trees.

"No," said Trey. "You need to look in a better place. I will take you to a store. It's a food store. You can look at the food. Maybe you will see mish."

PLACES TO LOOK FOR MISH:

~~THE GROUND~~

BINGO!
~~THE TREES~~
→ THE FOOD STORE

"No, we won't," said Neg.

"Maybe we will," said Poz.

"Come with me," said Trey. He walked away. Max went with him. The Toozers came too.

Soon they all came to the road. Trey looked at the twins. He could not take them into a store. People would stare.

"You must change," said Trey. "There cannot be three Treys. And you cannot be dogs."

"Okay," said Poz. "But we need to see someone. We can only become things we see."

Trey saw some signs. The signs were next to the road. They were ads for stores. The Toozers looked at one ad. Then they shimmered. They stretched. They changed.

They became two clowns. They were tall. They had white faces. They had bushy red hair. They had yellow clothes. Each clown had an M. The M was on their shirts. A car drove by. It honked its horn. Trey shook his head.

A PAIR OF CLOWNS

4
TWINS

"No," said Trey. "That is not good."

The clowns looked at a new ad. They shimmered. They stretched. They changed. They became two old men. They had white hair. They had little white beards. They wore glasses. They held pails. The pails held fried chicken. Trey shook his head.

"Try again," said Trey.

The old men looked at a new ad. It showed

a tall boy. He was playing soccer. He had a red can of soda. He was grinning. The old men shimmered. They stretched. They changed. They became tall boys. They wore soccer clothes. They held red cans. They had big grins.

TRANSFORMATION
← STAGE

"Not soccer players!" said Trey. "Try again."

"We are tired," said Poz.

"Yes," said Neg. "No more changes."

Trey sighed. Soccer made him think of Mr. Dean. And the science fair.

"We will look for mish now," said Poz. He started walking.

"Yes," said Neg. "The yeets are getting weak." He walked with Poz.

Trey and Max ran up. They walked into town.

Soon Trey saw Ben. Ben was his friend. Ben came up to Trey.

"Hi, Trey," said Ben. "Who are your friends?"

Poz started to talk. "We are Tooz—"

"They are visitors," said Trey. He talked loudly. He glared at Poz. "Their parents are at my house. We're going to Food Circus."

"Cool," said Ben. He looked at the Toozers. "You really look alike," he said.

"Yes," said Poz. "On Tooze, all—" Trey talked again.

"They are twins," said Trey. "Isn't that funny? See you later, Ben." Trey pulled Poz and Neg. He pulled them down the street.

"Don't talk," he said.

"Why not?" asked Neg.

"People will be upset," said Trey. "Here comes someone else. Don't talk to her."

A little girl walked up. She had on jeans. She had on a green shirt. She had a pony tail.

"Hi," said the girl. "You are twins. Where are you from?"

"From out of town," said Trey.

He pulled the Toozers some more. The girl walked with them. She petted Max.

"What are your names?" she asked the twins.

"They are Tim and Tom," said Trey. "Now go away. We are in a hurry."

Trey pulled the Toozers faster. He did not like the girl. He wanted her to go away. The girl stopped walking. She watched them walk away.

HER SUSPICIOUS EYES

"Come on," said Trey to the Toozers. "We will be there soon."

"Can we talk now?" asked Poz.

"Okay," said Trey. "But be careful what you say."

They got to the store. Max had to stay outside. Trey tied his leash to a pole. Then he opened the door. The Toozers went in. Trey looked back. The girl was still watching.

5
LOOKING FOR MISH

Trey went in the store. Oh no! Where were Poz and Neg? He didn't see them!

Trey walked around the store. He looked down each row. He saw two women. They both had handbags. They both had blue hair. They looked like twins. Trey walked up to them.

"Poz?" he asked softly.

"We are looking for mish," said one woman.

"We need mish for the yeets," said the other woman. Trey grinned. He had found them. But why were they women?

"Why did you change?" asked Trey.

"We don't know," said one woman.

"We just did," said the other woman.

"Well, change back," said Trey. But the Toozers didn't. They kept looking for mish.

One woman picked up an apple. She bit into it.

"Not mish," she said.

CRUNCH!

← TOOK A HUGE BITE

The other woman grabbed a banana. She bit into it.

"Not mish," she said.

"Stop," said Trey. "This is a store. You have to buy the food first."

Trey looked around. He needed a place to hide the food. He found a trash can. He took the food with bites. He put it in the trash can. Then Trey looked for the women. But they were gone.

"Not again," said Trey. He walked around the store. He looked for the two women. Soon he saw two carts. Each cart held a baby. Each baby had a bib. Each bib had a duck. Trey went to one baby.

MAMA!

"Neg?" he asked softly.

The baby had some salt. "Is this mish?" asked the baby.

The other baby tasted the salt. "No," said the other baby. "Not mish."

"You can't be babies," said Trey softly. "You must change now." He began to push the carts.

"Hi again," said a voice. It was the little girl. The one with the pony tail.

"Those are cute twin babies," she said.

"Go home," said Trey. "Your mom wants you." He pushed the carts fast.

BURNING RUBBER

"Change now," he said softly to Poz and

Neg. He looked behind him. The girl was gone. He looked at the carts. The Toozers were gone. Two men stood there. They had white aprons. They had plastic gloves.

"No more changing," said Trey. "You are making trouble."

"We are looking for mish," said one man.

"We must find it," said the other.

The men walked away. Trey hit his head with his hand.

"Hi, Trey," said a voice. It was Mr. Dean. He was shopping for food.

← AND THIS

"Uh, hi," said Trey. He looked for the men with aprons.

"How's that science idea coming?" asked Mr. Dean. "Don't forget. It's due Monday."

"I know," said Trey.

"No mish in this store," said a voice. Trey turned. He saw the two soccer players. They held red cans.

"What did he say?" asked Mr. Dean.

"Nothing," said Trey. "See you later, Mister Dean."

Trey grabbed the Toozers. He pulled them away. He was upset. The Toozers needed mish. He needed a science idea. What could he do? He looked at the Toozers. Maybe he could think of an idea about twins.

"Where are the babies?" asked a voice. It was the little girl again.

"What babies?" asked Trey. Then he remembered. "Oh," he said. "They weren't mine. Their mom took them."

The girl looked at the soccer players.

"Why are you in the store?" asked the girl. "Do you need something?"

Poz put his hand on Neg's mouth. Neg put his hand on Poz's mouth. Trey nodded at them.

"No," said Trey. "We don't need anything. We are going." He pulled the Toozers. He walked fast. He had to lose the girl. She asked too many questions.

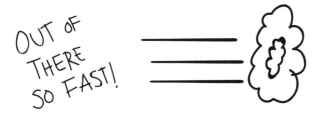

6
THE GIRL

Trey walked out of the store. He pulled the Toozers out. Trey tapped his finger on his chin. He was thinking.

"This idea is not working," said Trey. "We won't find mish in a store. There is too much food."

"But we need mish," said Poz.

"We don't want to stay on Earth," said Neg.

"I know," said Trey. He untied Max. "I have a better idea. Come with me."

Trey led Max and the Toozers. They walked out of town. Trey looked back. He looked for the girl. But he did not see her. *Good*, thought Trey.

"Where are we going?" asked Poz.

"To your ship," said Trey. "I need a clue. A clue for what mish is."

"There are no clues in our ship," said Neg.

"Yes, there are," said Trey. "There are smells. I will smell the mish tank. Then I will know about mish."

TREY HAS
A SENSITIVE
NOSE ↪   ↙FRECKLES

They walked into the woods. Max ran. He did not like being tied up. He stuck his nose in some leaves. He stuck his nose in the dirt. He sniffed a slug. He sniffed a snail.

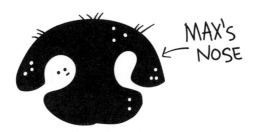

MAX'S NOSE

"Come on, Max," said Trey. "Stay with us."

As they walked, Trey was thinking. He was thinking about his science idea. Maybe he could study slugs. Or snails. Or why dogs stick their noses into everything. Soon they were at the ship.

"Here we are," said Poz. "I will get the mish tank."

Poz went in the ship. He came out. But he had the yeets bin instead.

"Look at the yeets," said Poz. "They look bad. They look sick."

"Oh no," said Neg. "We will have to stay on Earth."

"Earth is okay," said Poz. "We might like it."

"No," said Neg. "I want to go home."

Trey shook his head. He put his hands on his hips. He frowned.

"Get the mish tank," he said. "We have to fix it."

CLOSE-UP OF YEETS

Poz put the yeets bin down. He went back in the ship. Trey looked at the yeets. They moved very slowly. Max sniffed the yeets. Max sneezed.

Trey watched the yeets blow around. They took a long time to move back into a pile. Then Poz came out of the ship. He had the mish tank.

"Let me smell it," said Trey.

Poz gave him the tank. Trey looked for some mish. But there was none. Then Trey smelled inside the tank. It smelled good. It made him think of something. What was it?

Then Max started barking. He ran into the woods.

SOMETHING IN THE BUSHES!

"What is it?" asked Neg.

"We should go see," said Poz.

The Toozers shimmered. They stretched.

They changed into copies of Max. They started to follow Max. But someone popped out from the bushes. It was the girl from the store.

"I knew it!" she said. "You're Toozers!"

7

MORE TWINS

Trey's mouth fell open. He looked at the girl.

"What?" he said. "What did you say?"

The girl didn't look at Trey. She looked at the dogs.

"Change!" she said. "You cannot be dogs. I need to talk to you two."

TRANSFORMING... AGAIN.

The Toozers shimmered. They stretched. They changed back into soccer players. Trey watched the girl.

"Who are you?" Trey asked. "How do you know about Toozers?"

The girl looked at the tall boys. She looked mad. The boys sat down. They hung their heads. They looked sad. Then the girl looked at Trey.

"I'm Kem," she said. But then she stopped.

Max was barking again. He had found something. He came out of the woods. He was pushing a girl. She wore a green shirt. She had a pony tail. She looked like Kem. In fact, they were twins.

Trey put his hands on his hips. "You are twins too?" said Trey. "That is too odd. What is going on?"

NOT A HAPPY CAMPER

The new girl stood by Kem. She was holding something. It was small and yellow. It looked like a phone. She pointed it at the boys.

"We are Toozers," said Kem. "This is my twin. Her name is Fiz."

MORE TWINS?!

Trey looked at the girls. They were little. But they acted bossy. Trey looked at the boys. They were tall. But they acted scared.

"Why are you here?" asked Trey. "Did you crash?"

"No," said Kem. "We came here to study Earth."

Fiz nodded.

"What do you mean?" asked Trey.

"We study the people," said Kem. "We want to know about them. But only some Toozers can come to Earth. These two cannot."

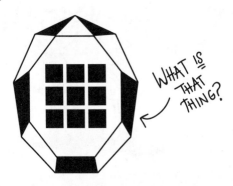

Fiz waved the thing at Poz and Neg. They hung their heads more.

"What is that?" asked Trey. He pointed toward Fiz. "Is it a phone?"

"It's a zapper," said Kem. "Fiz will zap them. Then other Toozers will know."

"Know what?" asked Trey.

"That they came to Earth. They shouldn't have come."

"Why?" asked Trey. "Why can't they come?"

"Toozers are a secret," said Kem. "Earth does not know about us. We blend in. But these two did not blend in. You saw them change. You know the secret. That is bad. We can't make you forget. But we can zap these two."

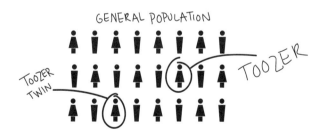

Kem looked at the boys. Poz and Neg had crawled behind the ship. They were peeking at her. Max was with them. He licked their faces.

TASTES LIKE RAISINS

"How many Toozers are on Earth?" asked Trey.

Fiz lifted one hand up high.

"Lots?" asked Trey. "But where do they all hide?"

"They don't," said Kem. "They blend in."

Trey shook his head. "How?" he asked.

"Have you ever seen twins on Earth?" asked Kem. "Twins that look the same?"

"Yes," said Trey. "There are lots of twins."

Kem smiled at Trey. Fiz winked at Trey. Trey's eyes opened wide.

"You mean all twins on Earth are Toozers?" he asked.

"No," said Kem. "But many are."

"Can I tell which ones?" asked Trey.

"No," said Kem. "They blend in very well. But these two did not." Fiz waved the zapper at the boys. "You saw them change," said Kem. "But we can't zap you. We have to zap them." Kem glared at Poz and Neg.

"They didn't want to land," said Trey. "Their ship broke. They crashed here."

"What do you mean?" asked Kem. "What broke on their ship?"

"They had no gas," said Trey. "The yeets stopped making gas."

LET'S RECAP
- YEETS EAT MISH
- THEN YEETS MAKE GAS
- GAS FUELS THE SHIP

The girls looked at the boys.

"Why?" Kem asked the boys. But they said nothing.

"There was no mish," said Trey. "The mish tank had a hole."

Kem and Fiz looked madder.

"So get more mish," said Kem. "Get more mish and go."

"We can't," said Trey. "We can't find any."

Kem looked at Trey. "Mish is easy to get on Earth," she told him.

Kem looked at Poz and Neg. "Get some now and leave!"

8

MISH!

Trey looked at the boys. Poz and Neg were shaking. But they did not talk. Trey spoke to Kem.

"But where?" he asked. "We don't know what mish is."

Kem looked mad. She grabbed the mish tank. She gave it to Trey.

"Sniff," she said. "What do you smell?" Trey took a big sniff. He liked the smell.

"I smell cake," he said. "And cookies and pie. It smells like our bake shop."

"That's because mish is sugar," said Kem. "On Earth mish is called sugar. Yeets eat sugar. Then yeets make gas. The gas makes our ships go."

THAT'S A LOT OF SUGAR!!!

Trey thought about this. Then he asked something. "How do you get so much sugar?" he asked. "You must use a lot."

"We buy it," said Kem. "The news says people eat too much sugar. But it's not people."

"You mean it's really the Toozers?" Trey asked.

Kem smiled at Trey. Fiz winked at Trey. Trey's eyes opened wide.

"So now you know," said Kem. Then she looked at the boys

"Get up," she said. "If you hurry, we won't zap you. Go get some sugar now."

But Poz and Neg didn't move. They were still shaking.

"I'll get it," said Trey. "I'll go to our bake shop. We have lots of sugar. Lots of things we bake use sugar."

"You have ten minutes," said Kem. "After that we won't wait. We will zap these two." Fiz waved the zapper at the boys again.

DO NOT WANT TO BE ZAPPED

51

Trey lifted the mish tank. It was pretty big. It would hold about twenty pounds of sugar. That was a lot. But Trey's parents had a big storeroom. There was lots of sugar in the storeroom. He put the tank down.

"I'll get your mish," he told the boys. "I'll be back fast. Repair the tank."

Poz peeked out. He used a small voice.

"Be very fast," said Poz. "The yeets look very weak."

"Be very fast," said Neg. "I don't want to stay on Earth."

"Be very fast," said Kem. "If you are late, we will zap these two. They will be in big trouble."

Fiz nodded.

Trey started running. Max ran close behind.

I THINK I SEE THE LIGHT!

9
ZAPPED

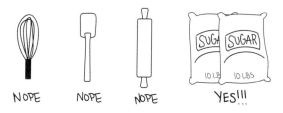

NOPE   NOPE   NOPE   YES!!!...

Trey ran fast. Max ran fast. In four minutes they were home. Trey ran inside. He ran through the kitchen. Then he ran into the bake shop.

In the storeroom he saw the sugar. He grabbed two ten-pound bags. He lifted them. Then he heard a voice.

"Trey?" said the voice. "What are you doing?" Trey's mom was standing in the

53

doorway. She looked at Trey. She looked at the two bags. She put her hands on her hips. Max stopped wagging his tail.

Oh no! thought Trey. What should he say? His mom wouldn't believe the real story. Trey thought hard. He needed an idea. (Why did he always need ideas?) Wait! He had it! He had the best idea!

"I need this sugar," Trey told his mom. "I need this sugar for school."

Trey's mom looked at him.

"You have an idea for the science fair?" she asked.

"Yes," said Trey. "But I will tell you later. Right now I need to run. Please?"

Trey's mom put her arms down. She smiled at Trey.

"Okay," she said. "Tell me at dinner."

Trey grinned at his mom. Max wagged his tail. Then they left. Trey had to get to the ship. He wanted to be in time. But the bags were big.

Twenty pounds was a lot of sugar. He couldn't run. He had to walk. He tried to walk fast. Would he be in time? Would the yeets be okay? Would Fiz zap Poz and Neg?

Trey walked fast through the woods. The big bags bumped his legs. Some of the sugar spilled. Max liked that. He licked up the sugar.

As Trey walked, he began to think. Did he have a science idea? Could he test sugar? He thought and thought. He walked slower and slower. Then he grinned. He had a great idea! He would tell his mom at dinner. His parents would be happy. Trey began to walk fast again.

At last Trey and Max got to the ship. Trey saw Kem and Fiz. The girls looked mad. He saw Poz and Neg. The boys looked sad. They were sitting on the ground. They were looking at their hands. They had large yellow Zs on their palms.

Neg looked at Trey. "You're too late," he said. "The yeets are dead."

10
THE IDEA

"What?" said Trey. He looked at Poz. Poz looked sad.

"Maybe they are," said Poz.

Trey looked at Kem and Fiz. The girls shook their heads. Trey hoped the Toozers were wrong. He looked in the bin. He looked at the yeets. They were very still. But Trey had to do something. He didn't want to give up. Not on the yeets. Not on Poz and Neg.

SO STILL

"I have an idea," said Trey. He opened a bag of sugar. He put some on the yeets.

Nothing happened.

Trey moved the bin into the sun. He looked at the yeets. They were so tiny. They were so still. Trey held his breath. Something moved! The yeets were moving!

"Look!" said Trey. "Look at the yeets."

Max came. He sniffed the yeets. He sneezed. The yeets blew around. Then they moved. They went back into a pile.

"I knew it!" said Trey. "The yeets are alive. They needed some warmth." The Toozers came to look.

Trey kept the bin in the sun. Soon all the yeets were moving.

"Will they be okay now?" asked Trey.

Poz nodded. He put the yeets bin in the ship. Neg put all the sugar in the mish tank. The tank was fixed

"The yeets are eating," said Poz. "They are making gas." Poz had a big grin.

"We don't have to stay on Earth," said Neg. He had a big grin too.

"Good," said Kem. "You can go now."

Then Poz looked sad. "We can't go back," he said. "We got zapped." He held up his hands. Trey saw the yellow marks.

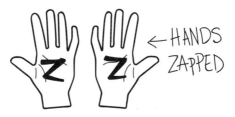

"Wash them off," said Trey.

Poz and Neg hung their heads.

"Can't," said Poz.

"They won't come off," said Neg.

Trey looked at Kem. "Can you help?" he asked. "They didn't mean to land here."

"But you know our secret," said Kem. "That is a bad thing."

Trey looked at Poz and Neg. They looked so sad. He looked at Kem.

"Can I promise?" asked Trey. "Can I promise I will never tell? Your secret will be safe."

Kem looked at Fiz. Fiz nodded. Kem looked at the boys. She sighed.

"Okay," she said.

Fiz lifted the zapper. She pushed a button. There was a flash. The boys looked at their hands. The zaps were gone. The boys jumped up. They shimmered. They stretched. They changed back into blobs.

"Thank you," said Trey to the girls.

Then the blobs got in the ship. They slid the door shut. Trey watched the ship take off. It was fast. Then it was gone. Trey turned to the girls. But they were gone. Only Max was there. And Max was busy. He was licking sugar off the empty bags.

It was two weeks later. It was the science fair. Trey was there. Little kids were there. Trey was showing them his work.

"Here is my test," said Trey. "I will show you what I did."

Trey had a bottle. He had some warm water. He put the water in the bottle. He added some sugar. Then he got a new thing.

"What is that?" asked one kid.

"This is yeast," said Trey.

"It looks like sand," said the kid.

Trey nodded. "Yes," he said. "But yeast is alive."

Trey put some yeast in the bottle. Then he got a balloon. He put the balloon on the top of the bottle.

"Now watch the water," Trey said. "Soon you will see bubbles. The bubbles will be in the water."

"Why?" asked a kid.

"The yeast is making gas," said Trey. "Now watch the balloon."

They waited. Then the balloon started to get big. It filled with gas.

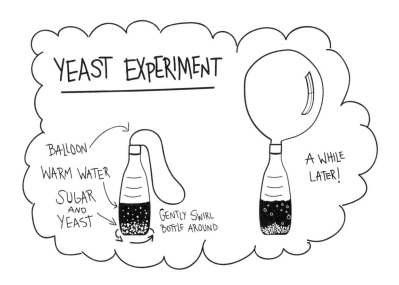

YEAST EXPERIMENT

BALLOON
WARM WATER
SUGAR
AND
YEAST

GENTLY SWIRL
BOTTLE AROUND

A WHILE
LATER!

"My parents have a bake shop," said Trey. "We use yeast a lot. It makes bread rise. Without yeast, bread would be flat. Yeast is tiny. But yeast is strong."

"What else can yeast do?" asked a kid.

"I don't know," said Trey. "But I want to learn about yeast. I want to make it stronger.

Strong yeast will make lots of gas. This gas could make things go."

"Cool," said a kid.

"Yes," said Trey. "One day I want to have very strong yeast. I will use it to make spaceships go!"

"You can't do that," said a kid.

Then Trey saw two girls. They were at the back. They were twins. The two girls nodded and winked at Trey.

"Yes, I can," said Trey. He grinned.